SKYLANDERS

CHAMPIONS

BLAME IT ON THE TRAIN

Written by:
RON MARZ and **DAVID A. RODRIGUEZ**

Art by:
SALVATORE COSTANZA

Colors by:
TOMATO FARM

Letters by:
DERON BENNETT

 Spotlight

ABDOPUBLISHING.COM

Reinforced library bound edition published in 2019 by Spotlight, a division of ABDO
PO Box 398166, Minneapolis, Minnesota 55439. Spotlight produces high-quality
reinforced library bound editions for schools and libraries.
Published by agreement with IDW.

Printed in the United States of America, North Mankato, Minnesota.
042018
092018

THIS BOOK CONTAINS
RECYCLED MATERIALS

Originally published as SKYLANDERS issue #6.

Library of Congress Control Number: 2017961397

Publisher's Cataloging in Publication Data

Names: Marz, Ron, author. Rodriguez, David A., author. | Costanza, Salvatore; Bowden, Mike; Cruz, David Garcia; Mazzara, Aurelio; Petrigno, Gaetano; Asaro, Massimo, illustrators.
Title: Champions / writers: Ron Marz and David A. Rodriguez; art: Salvatore Costanza; Mike Bowden; David Garcia Cruz; Aurelio Mazzara; Gaetano Petrigno; Massimo Asaro.
Description: Reinforced library bound edition. | Minneapolis, MN : Spotlight, 2019 | Series: Skylanders set 2 | Blame it on the train written by Ron Marz and David A. Rodriguez; illustrated by Salvatore Costanza, Mike Bowden & David Garcia Cruz. | Déjà vu all over again and again written by Ron Marz and David A. Rodriguez; illustrated by Aurelio Mazzara, Gaetano Petrigno, Mike Bowden & David Garcia Cruz. | I am legendary written by Ron Marz and David A. Rodriguez; illustrated by Massimo Asaro, Mike Bowden & David Garcia Cruz.
Summary: Join your favorite Skylanders heroes in these all-new comic book adventures! Jawbreaker races to save a train stolen by gear trolls, Déjà Vu advances to the final round of the Legendary Finals, and Blades learns the importance of teamwork during a dangerous mission.
Identifiers: ISBN 9781532142437 (Blame it on the train) | ISBN 9781532142444 (Déjà vu all over again and again) | ISBN 9781532142451 (I am legendary)
Subjects: LCSH: Skylanders (Game)--Juvenile fiction. | Monsters--Juvenile fiction. | Rescues--Juvenile fiction. | Teamwork (sports)--Juvenile fiction. | Fairies--Juvenile fiction. | Confidence--Juvenile fiction. | Magic--Juvenile fiction. | Comic books, strips, etc.--Juvenile fiction.
Classification: DDC 741.5--dc23

ABDO
Spotlight

A Division of ABDO
abdopublishing.com

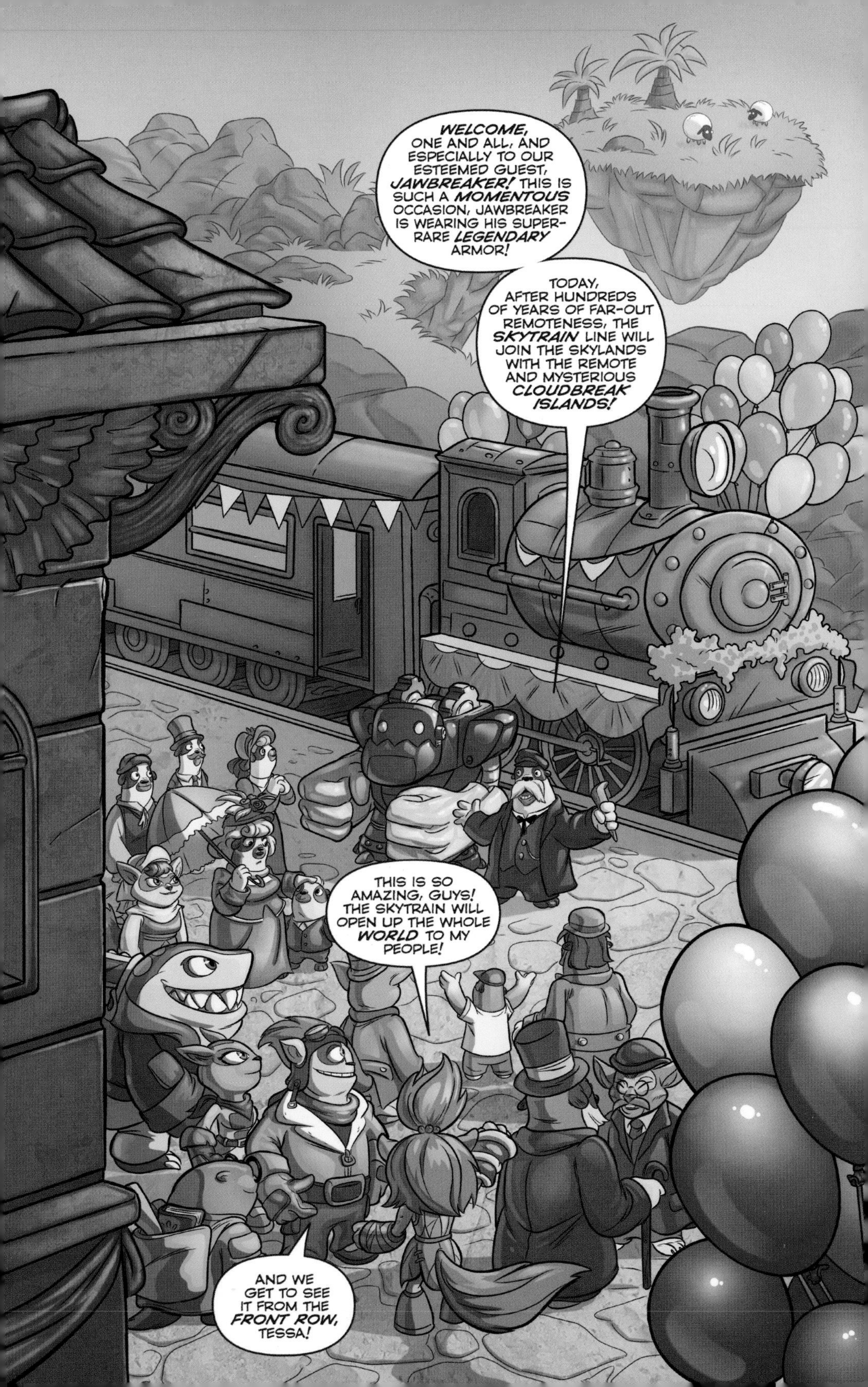
WELCOME, ONE AND ALL, AND ESPECIALLY TO OUR ESTEEMED GUEST, JAWBREAKER! THIS IS SUCH A MOMENTOUS OCCASION, JAWBREAKER IS WEARING HIS SUPER-RARE LEGENDARY ARMOR!
TODAY, AFTER HUNDREDS OF YEARS OF FAR-OUT REMOTENESS, THE SKYTRAIN LINE WILL JOIN THE SKYLANDS WITH THE REMOTE AND MYSTERIOUS CLOUDBREAK ISLANDS!
THIS IS SO AMAZING, GUYS! THE SKYTRAIN WILL OPEN UP THE WHOLE WORLD TO MY PEOPLE!
AND WE GET TO SEE IT FROM THE FRONT ROW, TESSA!

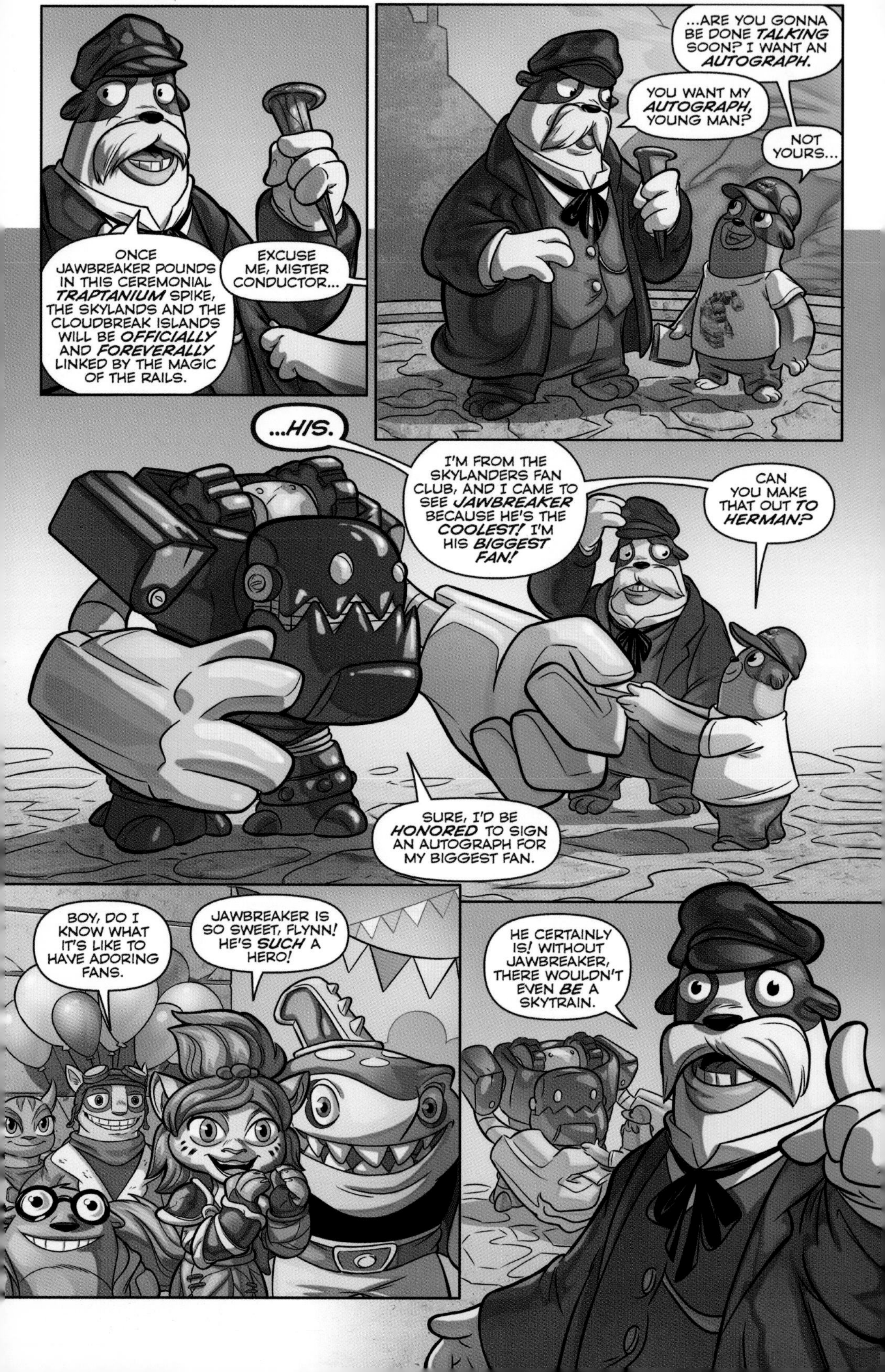
ONCE JAWBREAKER POUNDS IN THIS CEREMONIAL TRAPTANIUM SPIKE, THE SKYLANDS AND THE CLOUDBREAK ISLANDS WILL BE OFFICIALLY AND FOREVERALLY LINKED BY THE MAGIC OF THE RAILS.
EXCUSE ME, MISTER CONDUCTOR...
...ARE YOU GONNA BE DONE TALKING SOON? I WANT AN AUTOGRAPH.
YOU WANT MY AUTOGRAPH, YOUNG MAN?
NOT YOURS...
...HIS.
I'M FROM THE SKYLANDERS FAN CLUB, AND I CAME TO SEE JAWBREAKER BECAUSE HE'S THE COOLEST! I'M HIS BIGGEST FAN!
CAN YOU MAKE THAT OUT TO HERMAN?
SURE, I'D BE HONORED TO SIGN AN AUTOGRAPH FOR MY BIGGEST FAN.
BOY, DO I KNOW WHAT IT'S LIKE TO HAVE ADORING FANS.
JAWBREAKER IS SO SWEET, FLYNN! HE'S SUCH A HERO!
HE CERTAINLY IS! WITHOUT JAWBREAKER, THERE WOULDN'T EVEN BE A SKYTRAIN.

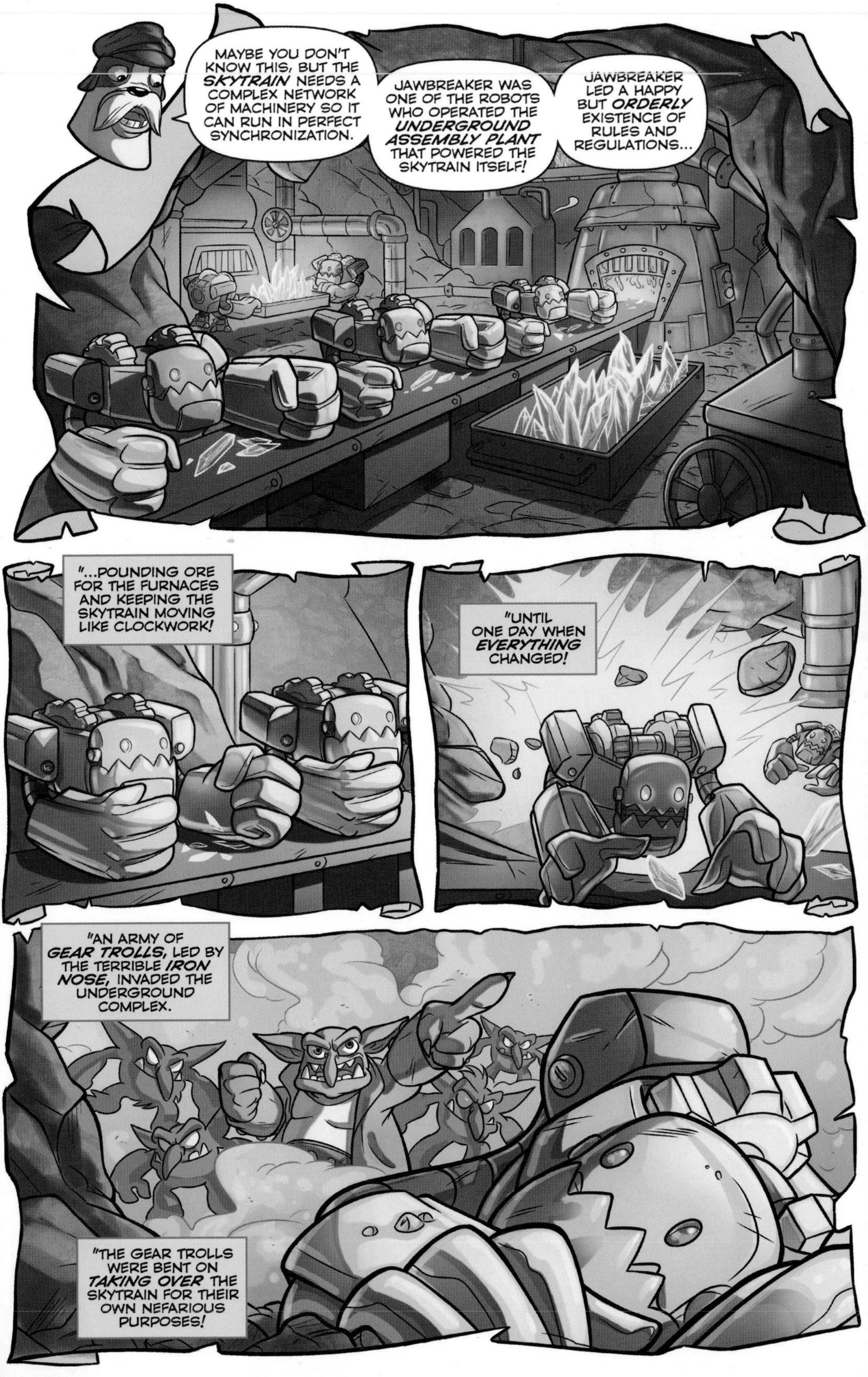
MAYBE YOU DON'T KNOW THIS, BUT THE SKYTRAIN NEEDS A COMPLEX NETWORK OF MACHINERY SO IT CAN RUN IN PERFECT SYNCHRONIZATION.
JAWBREAKER WAS ONE OF THE ROBOTS WHO OPERATED THE UNDERGROUND ASSEMBLY PLANT THAT POWERED THE SKYTRAIN ITSELF!
JAWBREAKER LED A HAPPY BUT ORDERLY EXISTENCE OF RULES AND REGULATIONS...
"...POUNDING ORE FOR THE FURNACES AND KEEPING THE SKYTRAIN MOVING LIKE CLOCKWORK!
"UNTIL ONE DAY WHEN EVERYTHING CHANGED!
"AN ARMY OF GEAR TROLLS, LED BY THE TERRIBLE IRON NOSE, INVADED THE UNDERGROUND COMPLEX.
"THE GEAR TROLLS WERE BENT ON TAKING OVER THE SKYTRAIN FOR THEIR OWN NEFARIOUS PURPOSES!

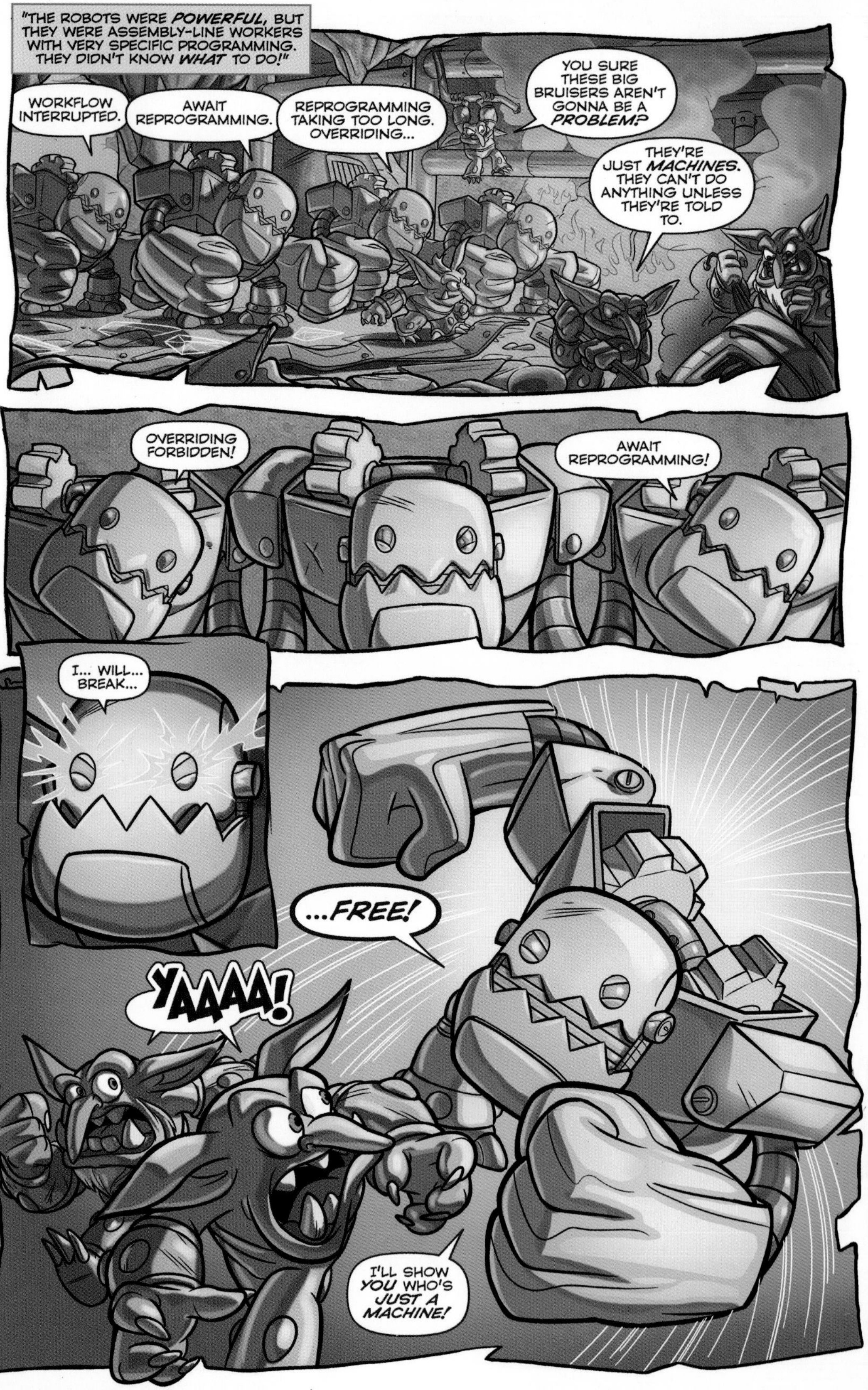
"THE ROBOTS WERE POWERFUL, BUT THEY WERE ASSEMBLY-LINE WORKERS WITH VERY SPECIFIC PROGRAMMING. THEY DIDN'T KNOW WHAT TO DO!"
WORKFLOW INTERRUPTED.
AWAIT REPROGRAMMING.
REPROGRAMMING TAKING TOO LONG. OVERRIDING...
YOU SURE THESE BIG BRUISERS AREN'T GONNA BE A PROBLEM?
THEY'RE JUST MACHINES. THEY CAN'T DO ANYTHING UNLESS THEY'RE TOLD TO.
OVERRIDING FORBIDDEN!
AWAIT REPROGRAMMING!
I... WILL... BREAK...
...FREE!
YAAAA!
I'LL SHOW YOU WHO'S JUST A MACHINE!

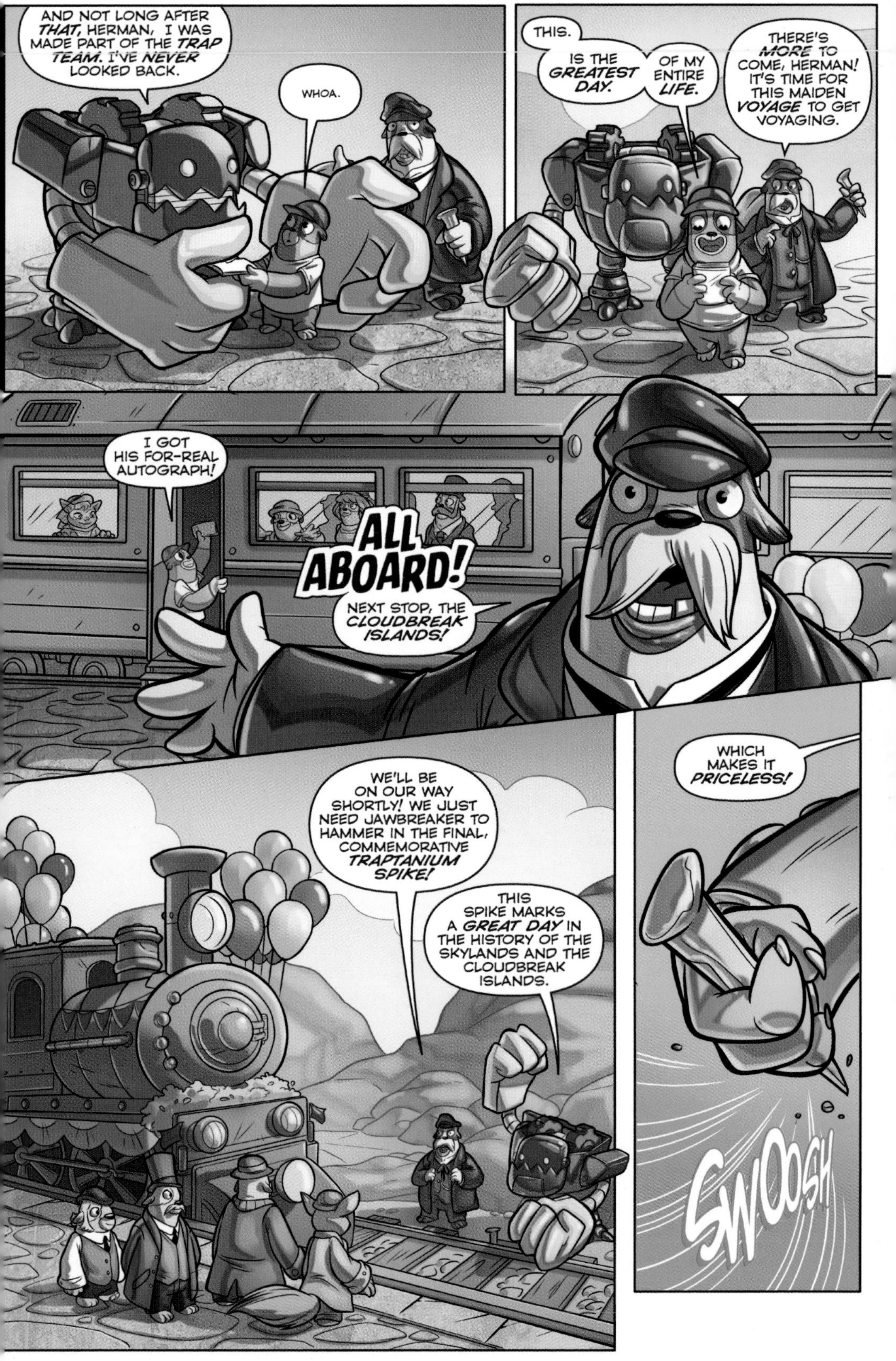
AND NOT LONG AFTER THAT, HERMAN, I WAS MADE PART OF THE TRAP TEAM. I'VE NEVER LOOKED BACK.
WHOA.
THIS.
IS THE GREATEST DAY.
OF MY ENTIRE LIFE.
THERE'S MORE TO COME, HERMAN! IT'S TIME FOR THIS MAIDEN VOYAGE TO GET VOYAGING.
I GOT HIS FOR-REAL AUTOGRAPH!
ALL ABOARD!
NEXT STOP, THE CLOUDBREAK ISLANDS!
WE'LL BE ON OUR WAY SHORTLY! WE JUST NEED JAWBREAKER TO HAMMER IN THE FINAL, COMMEMORATIVE TRAPTANIUM SPIKE!
THIS SPIKE MARKS A GREAT DAY IN THE HISTORY OF THE SKYLANDS AND THE CLOUDBREAK ISLANDS.
WHICH MAKES IT PRICELESS!
SWOOSH

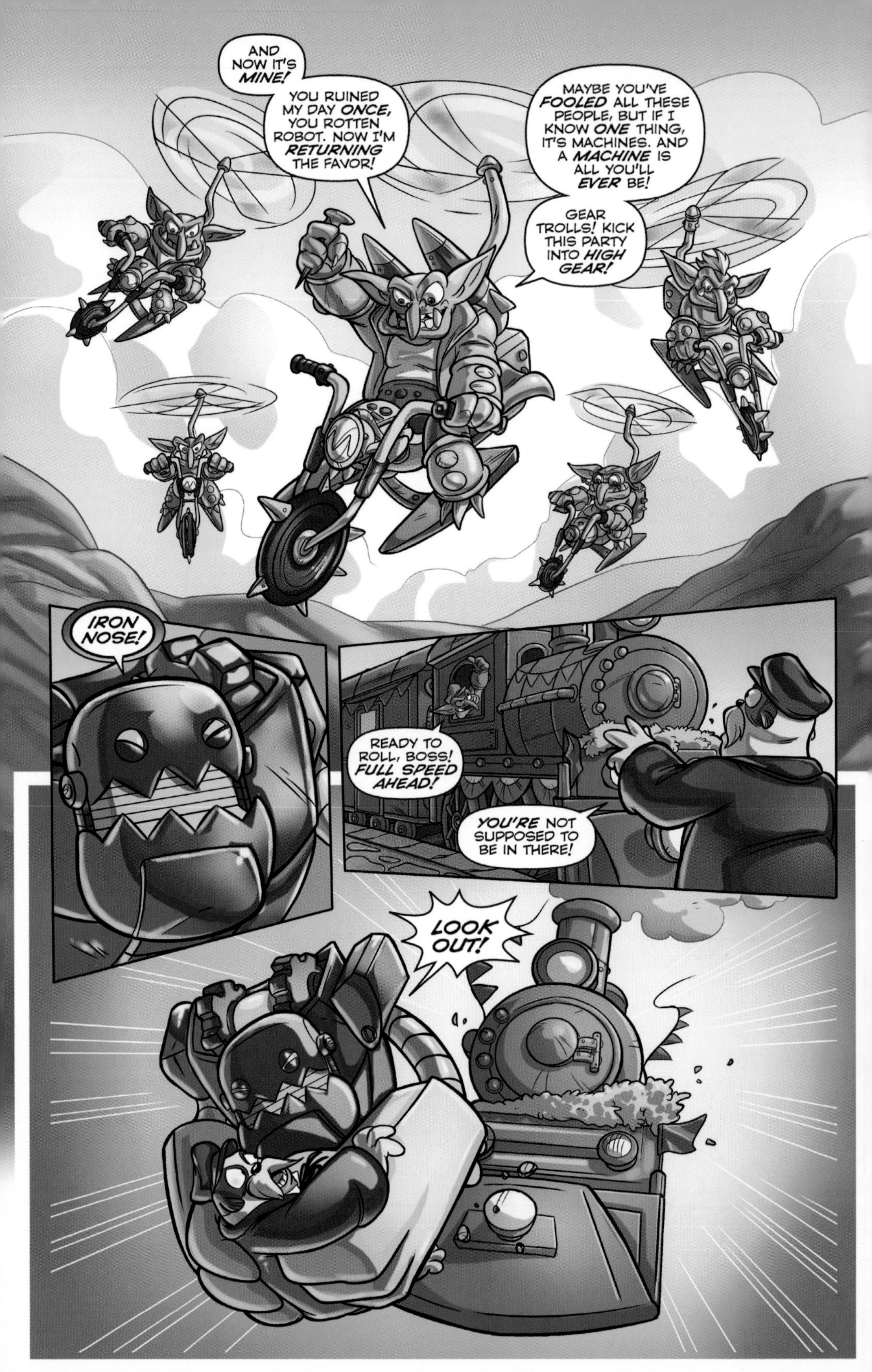
AND NOW IT'S *MINE!*
YOU RUINED MY DAY *ONCE,* YOU ROTTEN ROBOT. NOW I'M *RETURNING* THE FAVOR!
MAYBE YOU'VE *FOOLED* ALL THESE PEOPLE, BUT IF I KNOW *ONE* THING, IT'S MACHINES. AND A *MACHINE* IS ALL YOU'LL *EVER* BE!
GEAR TROLLS! KICK THIS PARTY INTO *HIGH GEAR!*
IRON NOSE!
READY TO ROLL, BOSS! *FULL SPEED AHEAD!*
YOU'RE NOT SUPPOSED TO BE IN THERE!
LOOK OUT!

MY *TRAIN!* MY LOVELY TRAIN!

AND THE *PASSENGERS!*

RIGHT, *SAVE* THEM TOO!

WAY AHEAD OF YOU!

THAT'S WHAT *I'M* TALKING 'BOUT!

I PULL OFF THE HEIST OF THE CENTURY *AND* GET TO RUB IT RIGHT IN THE NOSE OF THAT IDIOT AUTOMATON.

IF HE *HAD* A NOSE, I MEAN...

IRON NOSE!

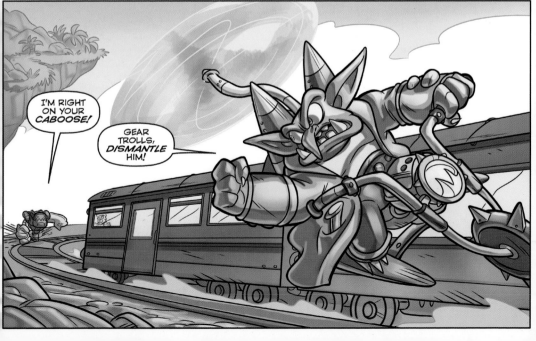

I'M RIGHT ON YOUR *CABOOSE!*

GEAR TROLLS, *DISMANTLE* HIM!

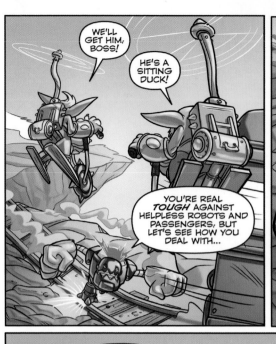

WE'LL GET HIM, BOSS!

HE'S A SITTING DUCK!

YOU'RE REAL *TOUGH* AGAINST HELPLESS ROBOTS AND PASSENGERS, BUT LET'S SEE HOW YOU DEAL WITH...

...A TRUE SKYLANDER!

CHEW ON *THESE,* JAWBREAKER!

CHOOM

CHOOM

IF IRON NOSE THINKS *YOU TWO* CAN STOP ME FROM SAVING THOSE PEOPLE...

...HE'S AS *DUMB* AS HE IS *UGLY!*

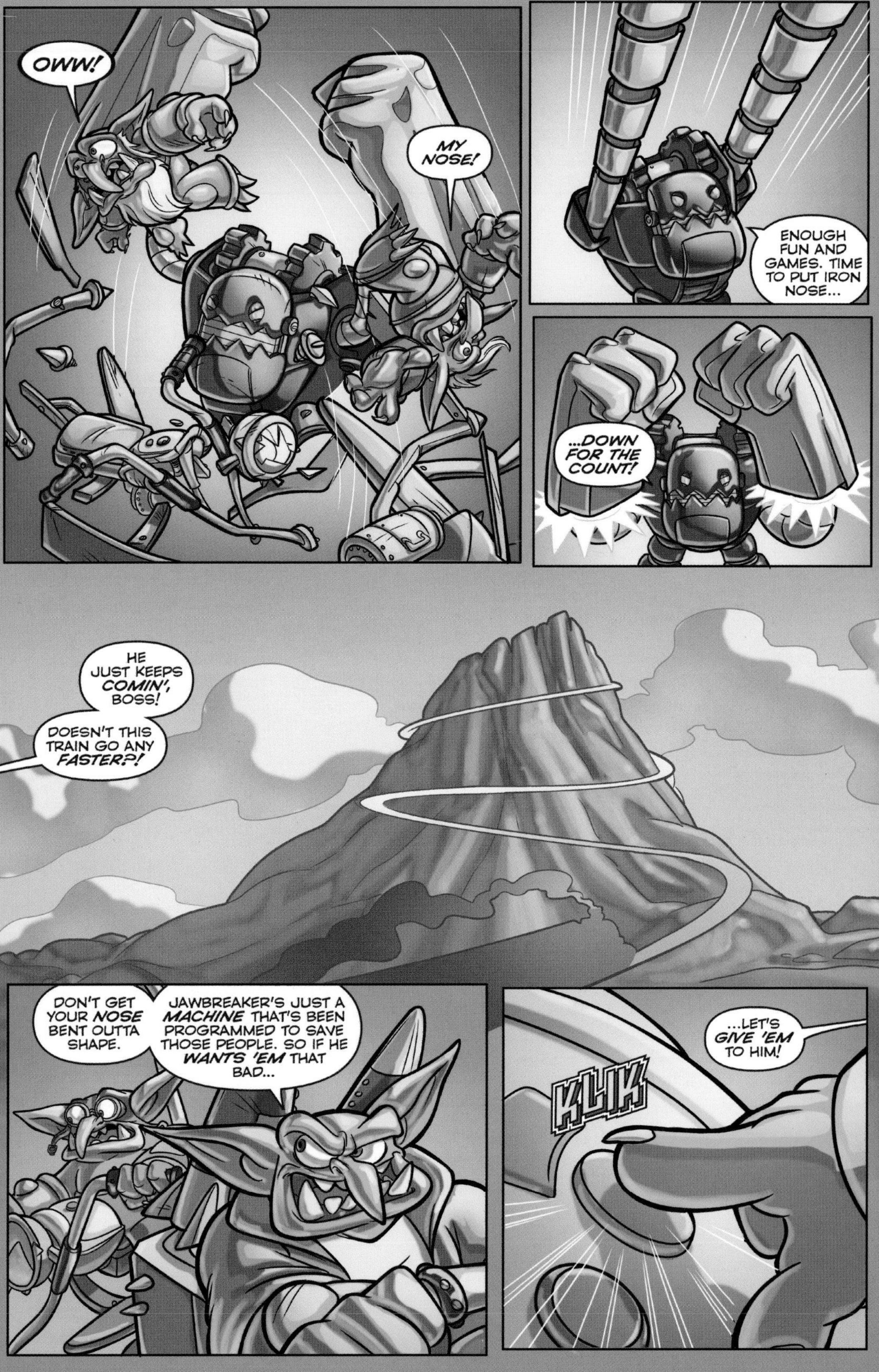
OWW!
MY NOSE!
ENOUGH FUN AND GAMES. TIME TO PUT IRON NOSE...
...DOWN FOR THE COUNT!
HE JUST KEEPS COMIN', BOSS!
DOESN'T THIS TRAIN GO ANY FASTER?!
DON'T GET YOUR NOSE BENT OUTTA SHAPE.
JAWBREAKER'S JUST A MACHINE THAT'S BEEN PROGRAMMED TO SAVE THOSE PEOPLE. SO IF HE WANTS 'EM THAT BAD...
KLIK
...LET'S GIVE 'EM TO HIM!

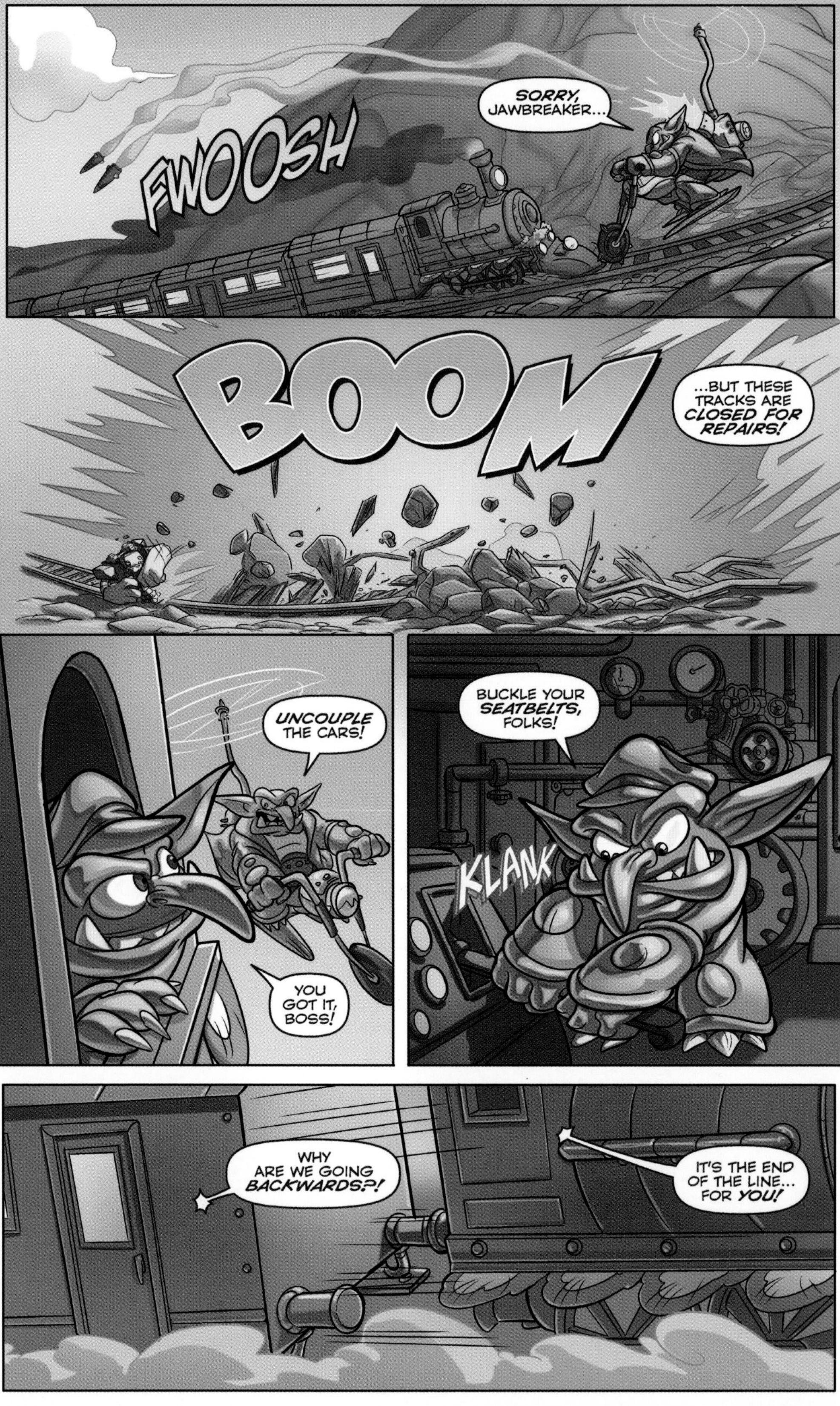
SORRY, JAWBREAKER...
FWOOSH
BOOM
...BUT THESE TRACKS ARE CLOSED FOR REPAIRS!
UNCOUPLE THE CARS!
YOU GOT IT, BOSS!
BUCKLE YOUR SEATBELTS, FOLKS!
KLANK
WHY ARE WE GOING BACKWARDS?!
IT'S THE END OF THE LINE... FOR YOU!

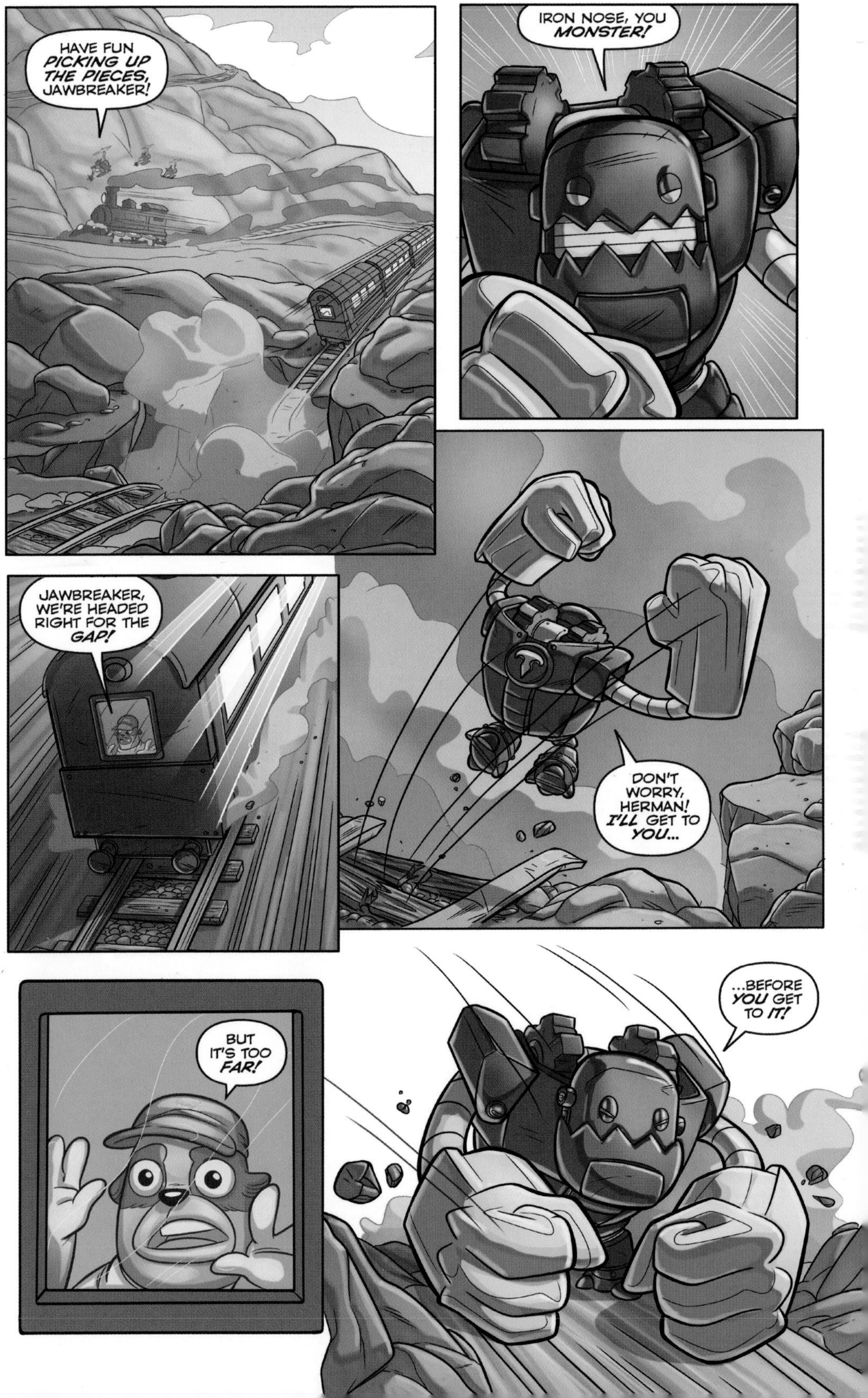
HAVE FUN PICKING UP THE PIECES, JAWBREAKER!
IRON NOSE, YOU MONSTER!
JAWBREAKER, WE'RE HEADED RIGHT FOR THE GAP!
DON'T WORRY, HERMAN! I'LL GET TO YOU...
BUT IT'S TOO FAR!
...BEFORE YOU GET TO IT!

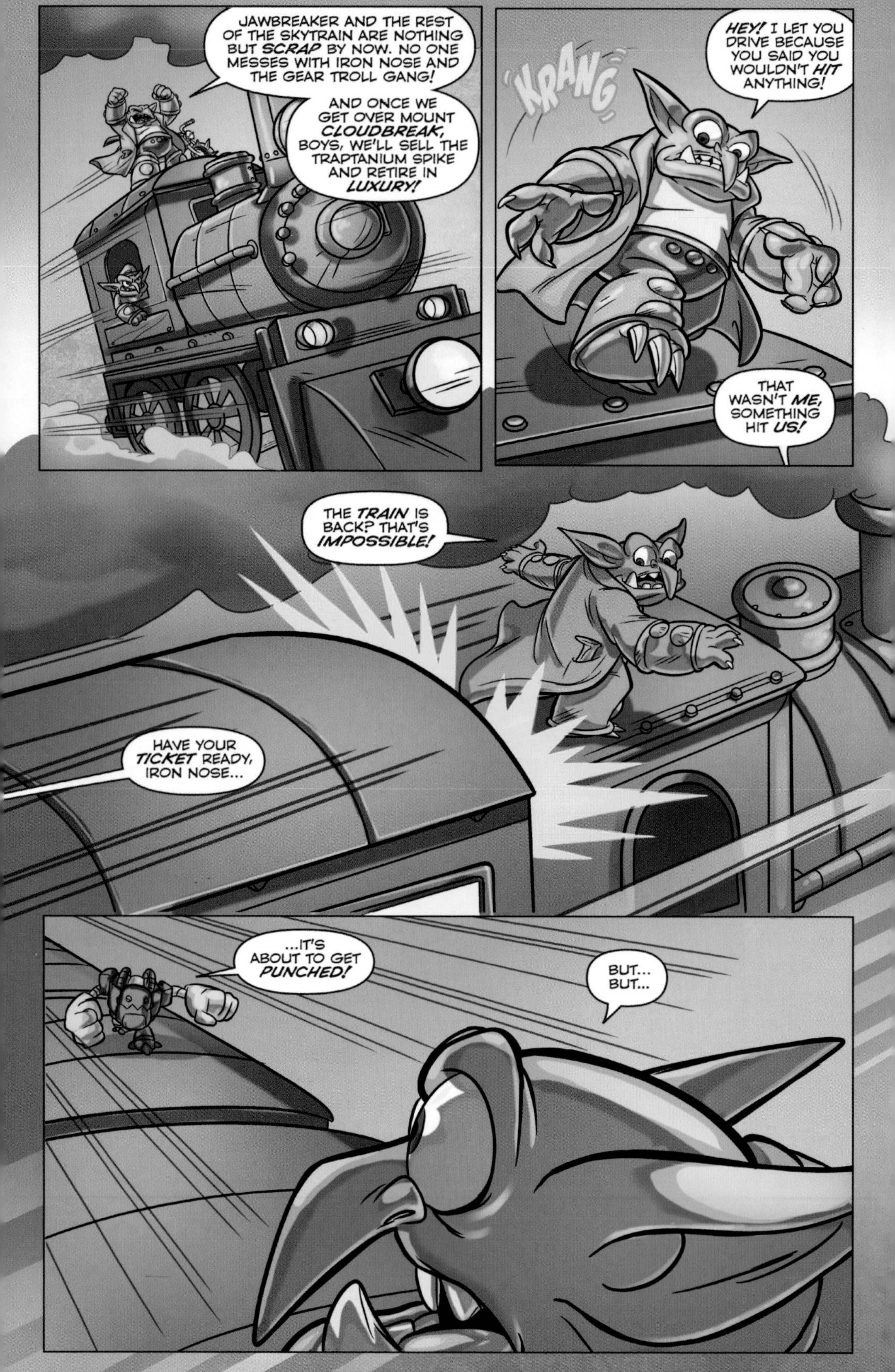

JAWBREAKER AND THE REST OF THE SKYTRAIN ARE NOTHING BUT SCRAP BY NOW. NO ONE MESSES WITH IRON NOSE AND THE GEAR TROLL GANG!
AND ONCE WE GET OVER MOUNT CLOUDBREAK, BOYS, WE'LL SELL THE TRAPTANIUM SPIKE AND RETIRE IN LUXURY!
KRANG
HEY! I LET YOU DRIVE BECAUSE YOU SAID YOU WOULDN'T HIT ANYTHING!
THAT WASN'T ME, SOMETHING HIT US!
THE TRAIN IS BACK? THAT'S IMPOSSIBLE!
HAVE YOUR TICKET READY, IRON NOSE...
...IT'S ABOUT TO GET PUNCHED!
BUT... BUT...

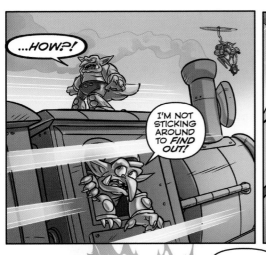

...HOW?!

I'M NOT STICKING AROUND TO *FIND OUT!*

YEAH, THAT SOUNDS LIKE A *GOOD IDEA...*

YOU'RE NOT GOING *ANYWHERE,* IRON NOSE...

...EXCEPT TO *SLEEP!*

NNGH!

POOM

LOOKS LIKE YOU HAVE SOMETHING THAT DOESN'T *BELONG* TO YOU...

...BUT I'LL MAKE SURE IT GOES BACK WHERE IT'S *SUPPOSED* TO BE.

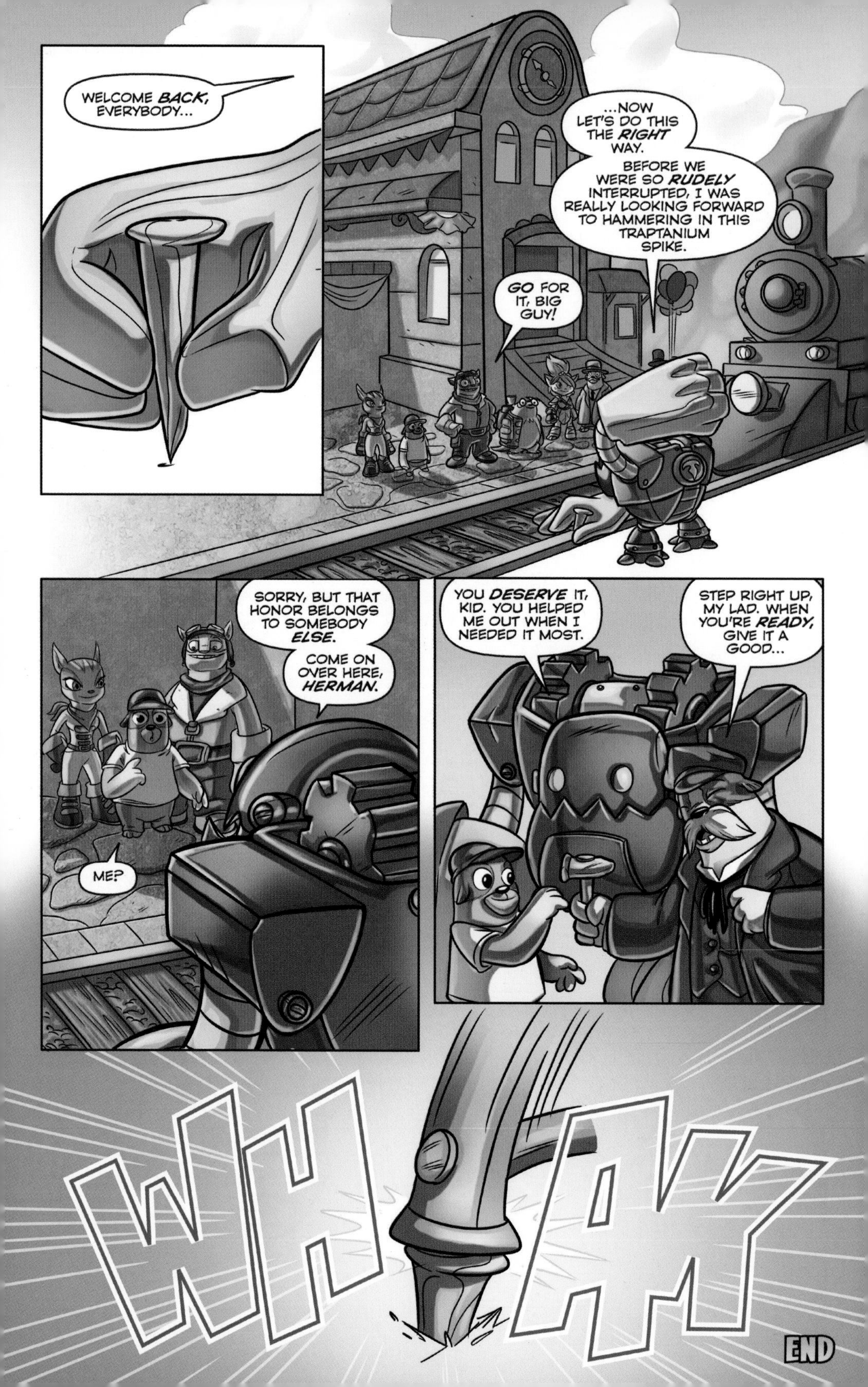
WELCOME BACK, EVERYBODY...
...NOW LET'S DO THIS THE RIGHT WAY.
BEFORE WE WERE SO RUDELY INTERRUPTED, I WAS REALLY LOOKING FORWARD TO HAMMERING IN THIS TRAPTANIUM SPIKE.
GO FOR IT, BIG GUY!
SORRY, BUT THAT HONOR BELONGS TO SOMEBODY ELSE.
COME ON OVER HERE, HERMAN.
ME?
YOU DESERVE IT, KID. YOU HELPED ME OUT WHEN I NEEDED IT MOST.
STEP RIGHT UP, MY LAD. WHEN YOU'RE READY, GIVE IT A GOOD...
WHAK
END

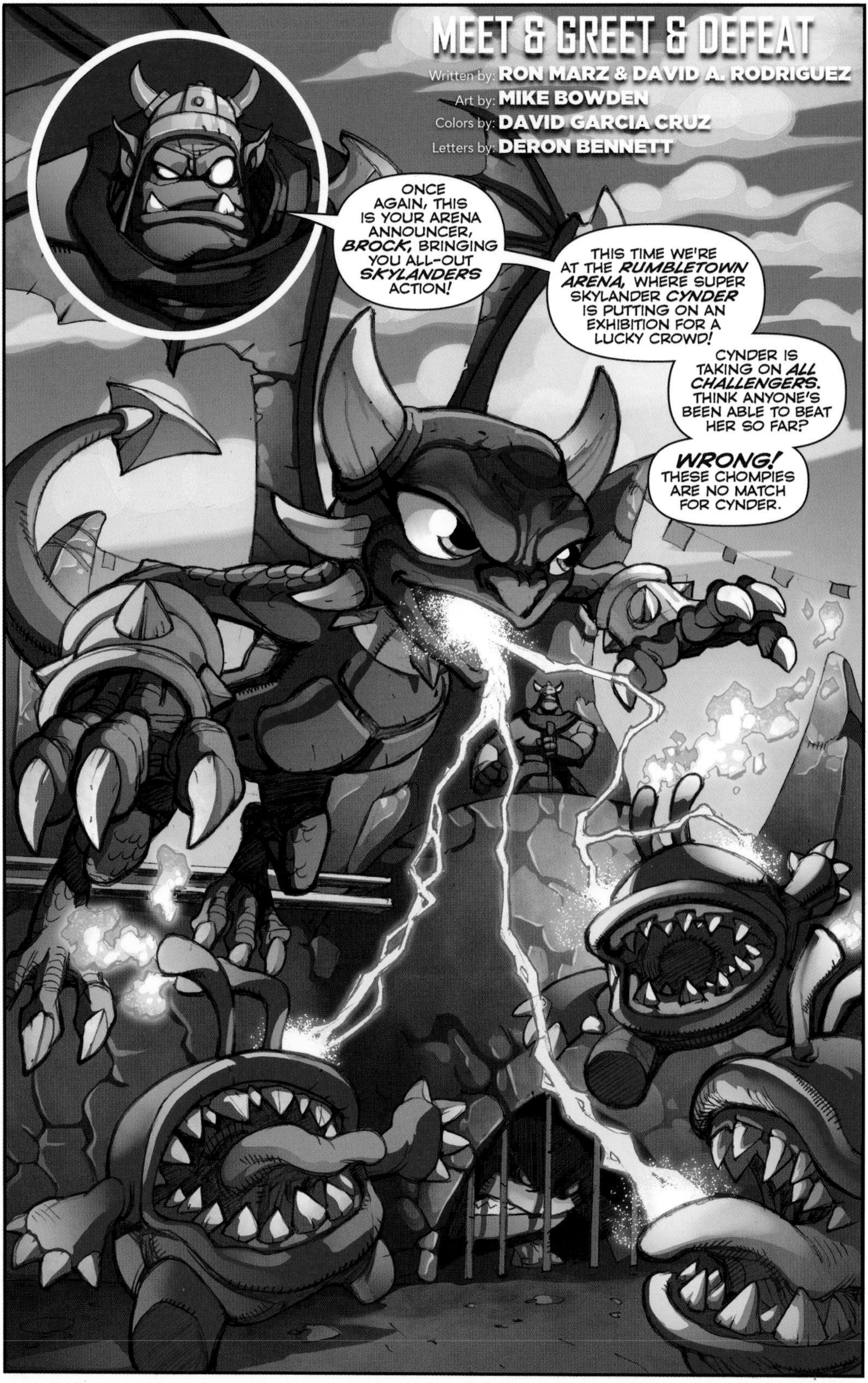
MEET & GREET & DEFEAT
Written by: RON MARZ & DAVID A. RODRIGUEZ
Art by: MIKE BOWDEN
Colors by: DAVID GARCIA CRUZ
Letters by: DERON BENNETT
ONCE AGAIN, THIS IS YOUR ARENA ANNOUNCER, BROCK, BRINGING YOU ALL-OUT SKYLANDERS ACTION!
THIS TIME WE'RE AT THE RUMBLETOWN ARENA, WHERE SUPER SKYLANDER CYNDER IS PUTTING ON AN EXHIBITION FOR A LUCKY CROWD!
CYNDER IS TAKING ON ALL CHALLENGERS. THINK ANYONE'S BEEN ABLE TO BEAT HER SO FAR?
WRONG! THESE CHOMPIES ARE NO MATCH FOR CYNDER.

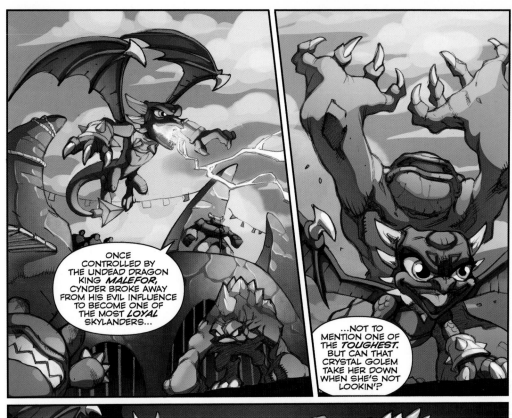

ONCE CONTROLLED BY THE UNDEAD DRAGON KING *MALEFOR*, CYNDER BROKE AWAY FROM HIS EVIL INFLUENCE TO BECOME ONE OF THE MOST *LOYAL* SKYLANDERS...

...NOT TO MENTION ONE OF THE *TOUGHEST*. BUT CAN THAT CRYSTAL GOLEM TAKE HER DOWN WHEN SHE'S NOT LOOKIN'?

WRONG! HE'S *NO MATCH* FOR HER *BLACK LIGHTNING!*

CYNDER EMERGES *VICTORIOUS*, AS ALMOST EVERYONE EXPECTED!

AS IF SEEING A SKYLANDER IN ACTION *UP CLOSE* WASN'T ENOUGH OF A TREAT...

...CYDNER WILL BE AVAILABLE FOR A *MEET AND GREET* OUTSIDE THE ARENA WITH LUCKY FANS.

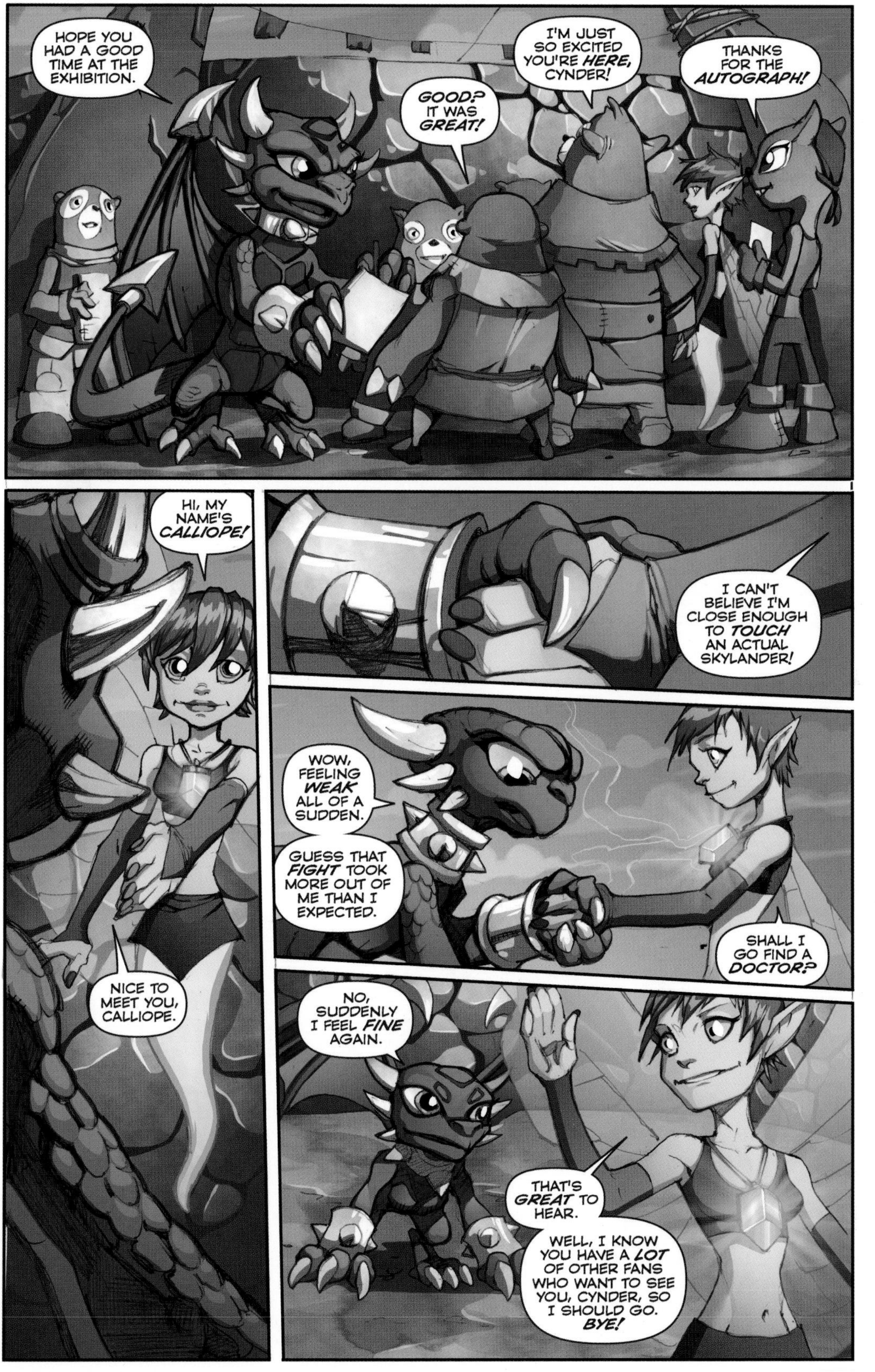
HOPE YOU HAD A GOOD TIME AT THE EXHIBITION.
GOOD? IT WAS GREAT!
I'M JUST SO EXCITED YOU'RE HERE, CYNDER!
THANKS FOR THE AUTOGRAPH!
HI, MY NAME'S CALLIOPE!
NICE TO MEET YOU, CALLIOPE.
I CAN'T BELIEVE I'M CLOSE ENOUGH TO TOUCH AN ACTUAL SKYLANDER!
WOW, FEELING WEAK ALL OF A SUDDEN.
GUESS THAT FIGHT TOOK MORE OUT OF ME THAN I EXPECTED.
SHALL I GO FIND A DOCTOR?
NO, SUDDENLY I FEEL FINE AGAIN.
THAT'S GREAT TO HEAR.
WELL, I KNOW YOU HAVE A LOT OF OTHER FANS WHO WANT TO SEE YOU, CYNDER, SO I SHOULD GO. BYE!

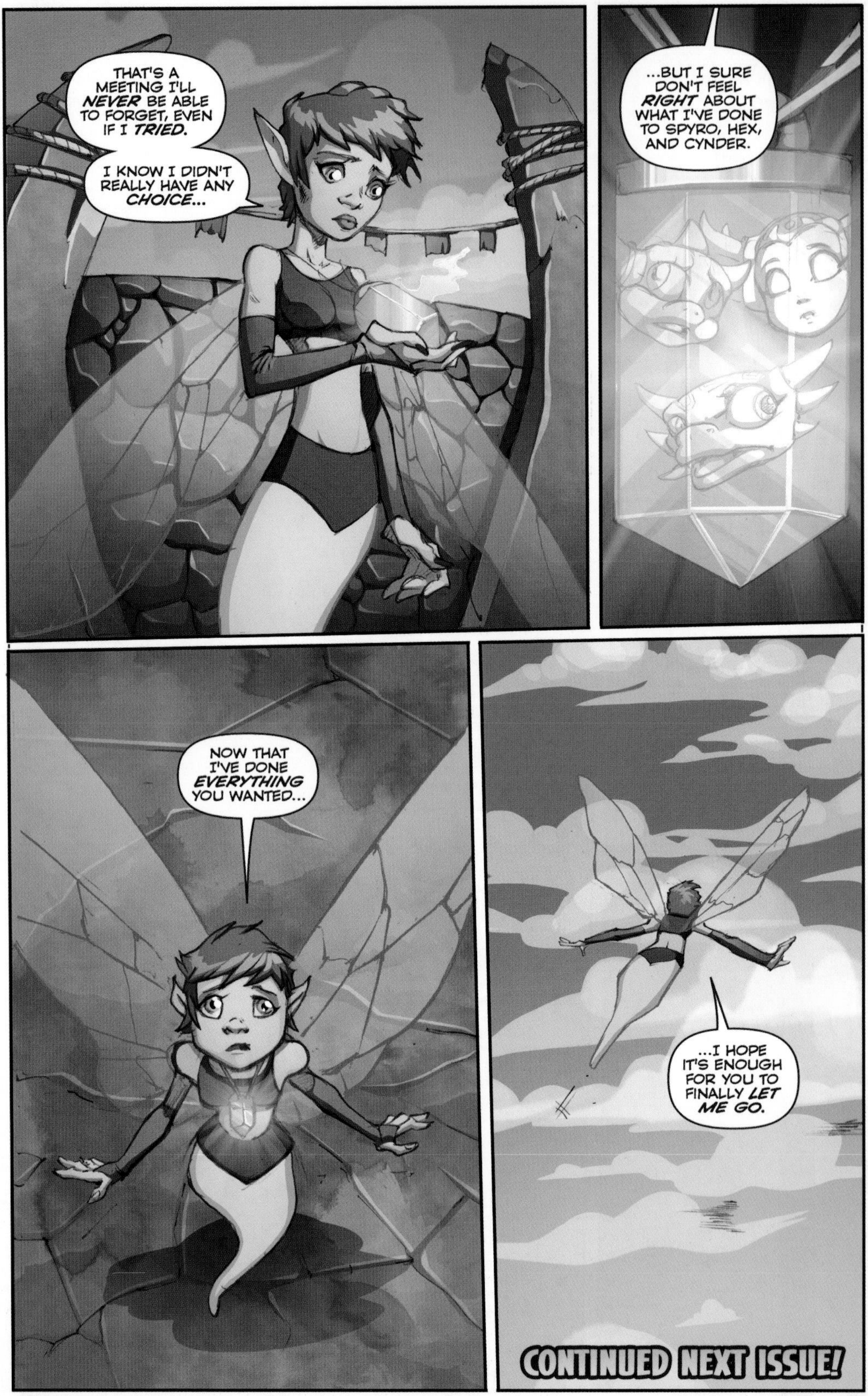
THAT'S A MEETING I'LL NEVER BE ABLE TO FORGET, EVEN IF I TRIED.
I KNOW I DIDN'T REALLY HAVE ANY CHOICE...
...BUT I SURE DON'T FEEL RIGHT ABOUT WHAT I'VE DONE TO SPYRO, HEX, AND CYNDER.
NOW THAT I'VE DONE EVERYTHING YOU WANTED...
...I HOPE IT'S ENOUGH FOR YOU TO FINALLY LET ME GO.
CONTINUED NEXT ISSUE!

SKYLANDERS™

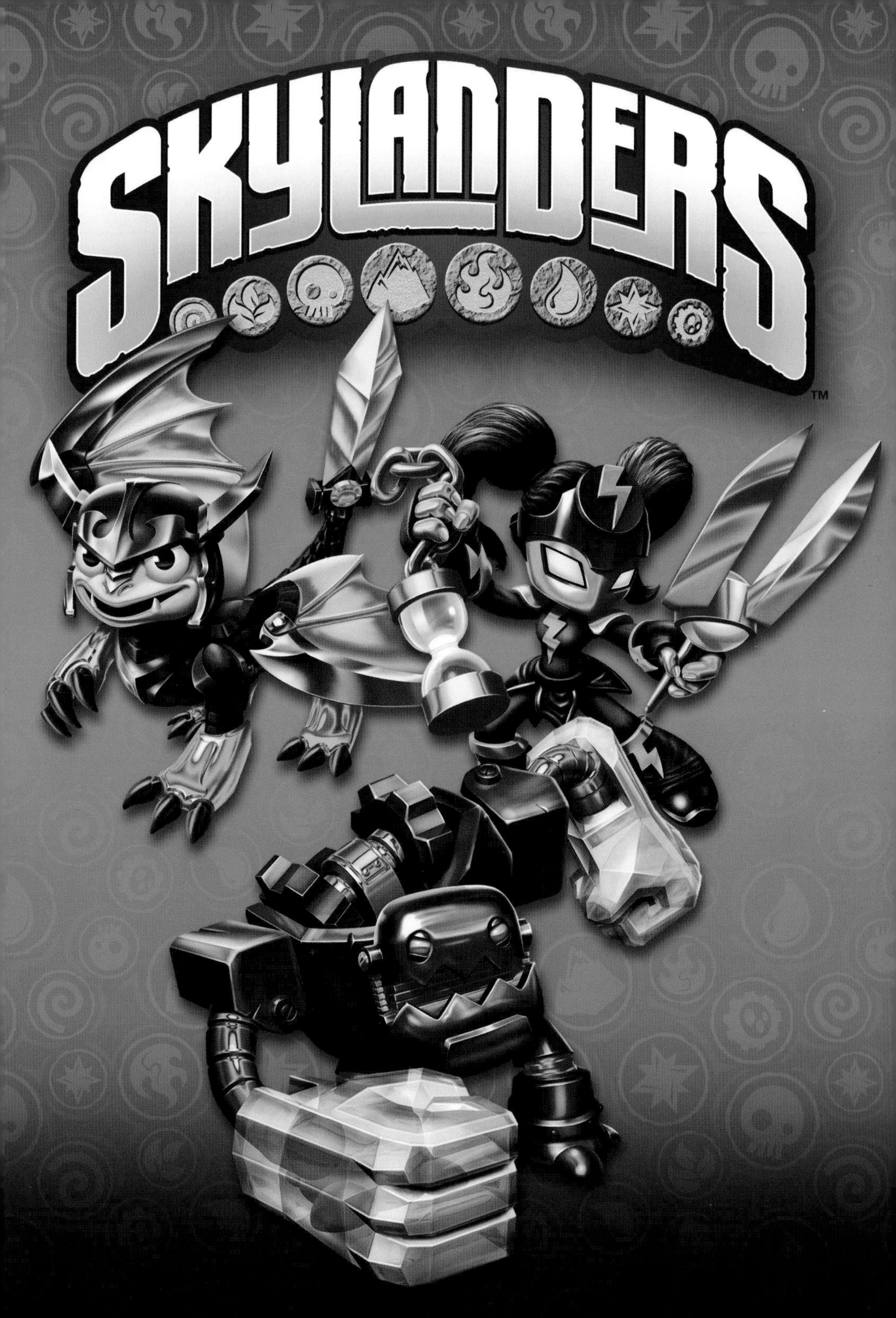

CHAMPIONS

SKYLANDERS™

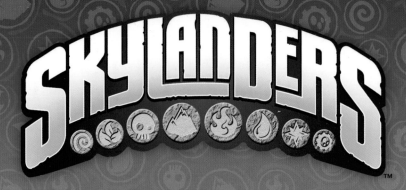

COLLECT THEM ALL!

Set of 6 Hardcover Books ISBN: 978-1-5321-4242-0

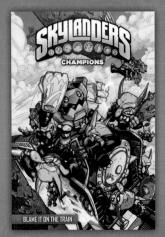

SKYLANDERS
CHAMPIONS
BLAME IT ON THE TRAIN

Hardcover Book ISBN
978-1-5321-4243-7

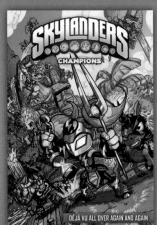

SKYLANDERS
CHAMPIONS
DÉJÀ VU ALL OVER AGAIN AND AGAIN

Hardcover Book ISBN
978-1-5321-4244-4

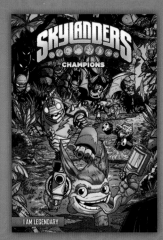

SKYLANDERS
CHAMPIONS
I AM LEGENDARY

Hardcover Book ISBN
978-1-5321-4245-1

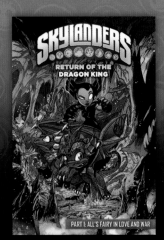

SKYLANDERS
RETURN OF THE DRAGON KING
PART 1: ALL'S FAIRY IN LOVE AND WAR

Hardcover Book ISBN
978-1-5321-4246-8

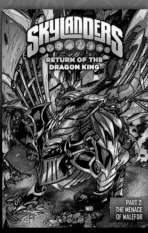

SKYLANDERS
RETURN OF THE DRAGON KING
PART 2: THE MENACE OF MALEFOR

Hardcover Book ISBN
978-1-5321-4247-5

SKYLANDERS
RETURN OF THE DRAGON KING
PART 3: REACH FOR THE SKY

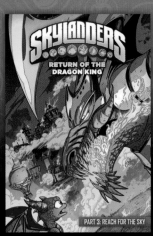

Hardcover Book ISBN
978-1-5321-4248-2